Max and Minnie

For Ben and Florence

First Published in 1992 by Magi Publications
55 Crowland Avenue, Hayes, Middx UB3 4JP

This edition published in 1994 by Magi Publications, for
School Book Fairs Ltd

Printed and bound in Belgium by Proost N.V. Turnhout

ISBN 1 85430 160 8

Magi Publications, London

Max and Minnie

Catherine Walters

One cold winter's night Max and Minnie were dozing by the fire, dreaming. Their whiskers twitched as they dreamed. Suddenly, in the corner of the room, behind the sofa, there came a little scuffling, rustling noise.

Max sat up. *Something* had disturbed him. Minnie yawned and stretched out in front of the fire.

"Mm –" she sighed. "Such a wonderful dream – mice galore, lots of juicy little sparrows . . ."

"Voles," added Max. "And shrews."

Both cats licked their lips greedily.

"I've never caught a mouse," said Max. "I've never even *seen* a real one."

Psst – what was that? A tiny scratching noise, as if a small animal were scurrying across the floor . . .

A mouse! Both cats sprang to their feet and the mouse was off in a flash, running back behind the sofa to its mousehole. The cats followed. "It's gone!" cried Max. "We'll never be able to squeeze down the mousehole after it."
But he was wrong. The mousehole, once mouse-sized, was now big enough for two rather plump cats.

"Come on!" cried Minnie. "What's stopping us now?"

The mousehole looked very dark and mysterious. The two cats padded along, until suddenly –

"Max!" cried Minnie. "There's a wood out here!"

"How can there be?" said Max. "We live in the middle of town!"

Both cats poked their noses out of the hole and blinked.

They were surrounded by tall trees. The wind rustled, filling their nostrils with wild smells of fresh rabbit and mice.

"It must be a magic mousehole," said Max.

"Max, look!" whispered Minnie. "What *are* they?"
Through the undergrowth gleamed thousands and thousands of eyes.
Max's tail lashed from side to side. "I bet they are everything we ever
dreamed of. Mice and voles, rats and shrews, rabbits and nice plump
birds . . ."
"Mm!" said Minnie, her mouth watering. "Where shall we begin?"
"Right here!" cried Max, taking off after a squirrel.

"Max, come back!" cried Minnie, but he had already disappeared through the trees. As Minnie sat in the middle of the clearing, wondering what to do next, she caught sight of a green object, hopping in front of her. It was too good to resist.

"GOTCHA!" she cried, snapping it up. Ugh! Her mouth was full of green and slimy frog. She spat it out. It didn't taste too good. So much for her first catch!

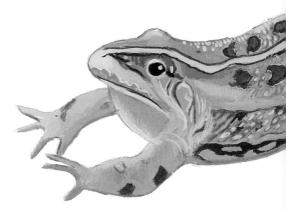

What was that? A sudden rustle in the bushes behind her.
"Max?" she called.
A flash of white teeth bared in a terrible snarl. It wasn't Max! It was a mink, though Minnie didn't know this. But she did know the creature was set upon eating her. With a yowl, she turned tail and sped off through the trees. The mink followed close behind.

It was pretty nasty being hunted.
She could almost smell the dreadful creature's hot breath.
"Oh *please* help me, someone," she wailed.
But Max wasn't there, and Minnie's heart was nearly bursting.
Then suddenly, there was a loud whirring of wings. A large owl
with fierce round yellow eyes, grasped her firmly in his talons
and flew with her into the air. Minnie felt a bit sick.
She didn't know if it was worse being chased,
or being dangled in the air by an owl who could eat her at any moment.
Then she spotted Max. He was stuck up a tree, mewing piteously.
"Oh, please let me down," she begged the owl.

When the owl heard Minnie speak, he hooted in surprise. He had thought she was a rabbit. Then he dropped her, and she fell, down and down, till she landed beside Max in the tree.

"I chased the squirrel up here," said Max. "But I can't get down again." Both cats peered through the branches. The tree was very tall, and its trunk was smooth and slippery.

"I wish we'd never gone down that mousehole," said Minnie. "I wish we'd stayed safely at home by the fire."

"Nothing's like it was in my dream," said Max.

It grew very cold and began to snow.
"We can't stay here," said Max. "We'll freeze to death."
So they gradually and carefully began to slither and slide down the
smooth trunk, until thump! they reached the bottom.
"Now we'll find the mousehole," said Minnie.
The two cats began to look forward to a warm fire, creamy evaporated
milk and a plate of cooked chicken livers.

But Max and Minnie were completely lost. The snow was fast covering all the woodland tracks. There were no nice plump mice, no voles, no birds. Just a white, cold, unfriendly wood.

"Yeouw," cried Max miserably.

And "Yeouw," replied a voice from the undergrowth.

It was a cat – a large, coarse-haired tabby with fierce yellow eyes.

"Lost, are you?" said the cat. "Looking for your mousehole?"

"Oh yes," said Minnie eagerly. "How did you guess?"

"I can recognise a town cat anywhere," he said. "I can see you're not rough, tough, wild cats. And it's not the first time a cat has come through the mousehole to the wet wild wood."

The two wet and hungry cats padded after the wild cat till they came to the clearing where Max had chased the squirrel. And there was their mousehole!

"Goodbye," they cried to their wild cat friend. He barely answered them. He was off through the trees, chasing a squirrel!

"I think," said Max in a small voice, "I think I prefer my food served up cooked on a plate."

In a couple of twitches of a cat's tail they were back in their very own sitting room.

Max and Minnie curled up thankfully in front of the dying fire. They were town cats really. It was all too frightening out there in the wet wild woods.

The next morning they looked for their mousehole behind
the sofa. It had completely disappeared.

PRINTED IN BELGIUM BY

proost
INTERNATIONAL BOOK PRODUCTION